The Garish Sun

Also by Craig Lancaster

Novels

600 Hours of Edward
The Summer Son
Edward Adrift
The Fallow Season of Hugo Hunter
This Is What I Want
Edward Unspooled
Julep Street
You, Me & Mr. Blue Sky (with Elisa Lorello)
And It Will Be a Beautiful Life
Northward Dreams

Short stories

The Art of Departure

Plays

Straight On To Stardust

THE GARISH SUN

a play in three acts by
Craig Lancaster

ISBN: 979-8-9903324-3-0

For the ink-stained wretches—those still standing up for the cause, and those who have granted themselves release.

The Garish Sun

Cast of Characters

Sonny Sturgis: Late thirties to early forties; editor of the *Sun* newspaper in an unnamed Montana town

Livingston Sloane: Late forties to early fifties; high-powered lawyer and owner of the *Sun*

Randi Hutch: Late twenties to early thirties; the *Sun*'s star reporter

Dexter Collins: Early twenties; former collegiate football star, now an aspiring journalist

Anna Sturgis: Mid- to late thirties; Sonny's estranged wife

Other Characterization Needs

Woman's voice: Ginger, unseen desk clerk (tech)

Man's voice: Dave Jennings, unseen press operator (tech)

Scene

Sonny's office at the *Sun*

Time

Present day

ACT ONE

SCENE ONE

SETTING: We are in the large office of SONNY STURGIS, the editor of the *Sun*, a newspaper in an unnamed Montana town. The office contains a desk strewn with papers, a large computer terminal in the corner atop the desk, and a large table in the middle of the room for sitdowns and impromptu conferences. Newspaper offices are traditionally junky, and this one is no different. Papers and coffee mugs are stacked around haphazardly. The office is accessible by a door, stage right.

AT RISE: SONNY STURGIS is alone in the office. He stands near the exit, and he flings darts at a board affixed to the far wall. The circular dartboard bears the smirking visage of a man maybe five to ten years older than SONNY. After SONNY exhausts his supply of darts into the board, he walks over, pulls the darts, carries them back to his spot, and begins a fresh round of throwing. As he's doing so, a buzzer sounds, causing a misfire on one of SONNY's throws. This frustrates him. He walks over to his desk and presses a button.

SONNY
Yeah?

WOMAN'S VOICE
Mr. Sturgis?

SONNY
Unfortunately.

WOMAN'S VOICE
(unaffected by the sarcasm)
Mr. Sloane to see you.

SONNY
(checking the clock on the wall near him)
What's he doing here at this hour?

WOMAN'S VOICE
I wouldn't know. Shall I send him back so you can pitch that question to him
yourself?

SONNY
Let's simmer down now, Ginger. Yeah, send him back.

*(SONNY disengages the intercom. He tucks in his shirttail. He checks his zipper and
makes sure it's up. He holds a cupped hand near his face and blows into it, then sniffs.
Unsatisfied with the result, he retrieves a stick of gum from a pocket, unwraps it, and jams
it into his mouth. He then goose-steps over to the dartboard, removes the darts—along with
the one he misfired, from the floor—and flips the dartboard over, revealing another picture,
this one of a well-kempt SONNY, a beaming little boy, and a strikingly beautiful woman,
posed as if for a holiday picture. SONNY then hightails it to his desk and throws the
darts in the top drawer, just as another man enters the glass cubicle. This is LIVING-
STON SLOANE. He's a large, tidy man, wearing high-end cowboy finery—everything
but the hat, which he holds by the brim. He's also the man on the other side of SONNY's
dartboard. He smiles when he sees SONNY and crosses the office, hand extended. SON-
NY stands but stays on his side of the desk and accepts the handshake glumly.)*

LIVINGSTON
(looking at the detritus strewn about SONNY's office)
Is there a place where I can sit down?

SONNY
Oh, sure. Somewhere in there.

(LIVINGSTON, perturbed, unearths a chair by removing items from it: overcoat, piles of newspaper, hat, gloves, etc. He lumbers into the seat, clearly a man used to more luxurious reposes. SONNY continues standing.)

LIVINGSTON
Sit down, Sonny.

(SONNY, hesitatingly, does as he is told.)

LIVINGSTON (cont.)
Surprised to see me?

SONNY
No.

LIVINGSTON
No?

SONNY
Surprise is a professional vulnerability, Livingston. I'd rather size up likelihoods. I'd surmise that the tomato you're running around with needs you in town for some reason, but that ended last year, didn't it?

LIVINGSTON
(reproachfully)
Sonny…

SONNY
So I'd say that puts two possibilities in play: One, you've met your quota this month for sending poor bastards into medical bankruptcy and made another small fortune in foreclosures—

LIVINGSTON
(verging on anger)
Sonny, knock it off…

SONNY
(standing)
Or—and this is probably it—you've finally found the nutsack to fire me.

(LIVINGSTON looks up, eyes flashing. SONNY feels the weight of the realization that he's correct in his assessment.)

SONNY
Jesus. No kidding?

LIVINGSTON
(grinning)
No kidding.

(SONNY slumps into his chair. LIVINGSTON rises from his.)

SONNY
Damn. It sure is a burden to be this right all the time.

LIVINGSTON
(beginning to pace and take measure of the space he's in)
Don't let it bother you too much, Sonny. Notwithstanding your pessimism about my nutsack—to use your crudity—I didn't come here this morning simply to fire you. Although let me be clear: I could have, and maybe should have, a long time ago. I would have been more than justified in doing so, believe me.

SONNY
(finding his vigor)
So why didn't you?

LIVINGSTON
Because Sonny Sturgis, Pulitzer Prize winner, however long in the tooth that bit of monumental luck has become, is of far more use to me and to this newspaper as the august and much-admired editor-in-chief than he is as a paragon of journalistic value who was unfairly cast out by a thin-skinned and vengeful owner who doesn't know ethics from an abscess in his ass. I believe that's your direct quote about me, yes? From your address to the Butte Press Club last year?

SONNY
Yes.

LIVINGSTON
You see, Sonny, you don't hold me in much regard—

SONNY

That's true.

LIVINGSTON

—and though I'm well acquainted with what you think of me, I choose to look past it. I think that makes me the better man.

SONNY

Nope. Just the more privileged man.

LIVINGSTON

It used to bother me a bit, I'll admit, because I thought it unfair and unfortunate. I think if you'd ever taken the time to get to know me—

SONNY

Yeah, no chance. I don't truck with cronyism. I don't truck with men who buy newspapers and use them as ATMs and, after they're bled dry, tax writeoffs. But that's just me. I have standards.

LIVINGSTON

As I say, it used to bother me. But no more. And now, it is simply academic. Today—that is, the paper that we throw on a diminishing number of lawns tomorrow morning—will be your last at the *Sun*. I will do you the favor of a handsome severance.

(LIVINGSTON reaches into his back pocket and produces a small stack of envelopes. He hands them across the desk to SONNY.)

LIVINGSTON

Yours is on top. The rest are for everyone else. Oh, see, I forgot the most important part: It's your last day and the *Sun*'s last day, too.

(SONNY flings the envelopes down on the desk in anger.)

SONNY

Goddammit, you can't do that.

LIVINGSTON

Oh, Sonny, not only can but did. It was remarkably easy, in fact. A couple of sitdowns with my tax lawyer, and it was done. Not that you care, but I'll have a tidy writeoff on the loss this year and a tidy profit on the sale of this downtown corner lot next year. It's just the sort of good fortune that made it easier for me to write those checks you just spiked.

(SONNY comes around the desk and gets in LIVINGSTON's face.)

SONNY
What a ghoul you are.

LIVINGSTON
But give me my due: I'm a generous ghoul who gives six months' severance.

SONNY
No. You're just a garden-variety ghoul. But a world-class son of a bitch.

LIVINGSTON
To-may-toe, to-mah-toe. Goodness, Sonny, if you continue in this vein, I don't believe I'll be able to write you a letter of recommendation.

(LIVINGSTON waits for more invective from SONNY and gets none as the realization of what has transpired sinks in. SONNY hangs his head and walks back to the other side of the desk. LIVINGSTON puts on his hat and prepares to leave.)

LIVINGSTON
Sonny, a word of advice.

SONNY
What?

LIVINGSTON
You'll be tempted to write an editorial denouncing me for this—after all, despite your clear disapproval of me, I've never stopped you from publishing anything—but I'd urge you to resist that temptation. And if you're thinking of springing another one of those investigations that have given me such heartburn over the years, better forgo that, too.

You see, I know more about what goes on here than you've ever given me credit for, and I can make sure a day's worth of newspapers go straight from the loading dock to the dumpster with the greatest of ease. That wouldn't be fair to our hardy little band of subscribers, who deserve a proper goodbye. Take this opportunity to give it to them, to thank the good people of this city for a good run, and be done with it. This newspaper, and my stewardship of it, of which you so vociferously disapprove, made you what you are, Sonny. Be graceful, for once. Show some appreciation.

SONNY
Fuck you.

LIVINGSTON
Very well, then. It's only advice. Whatever you do, make it quick.

SONNY
Why?

LIVINGSTON
Because I'll have a truck here at eight p.m. to load up the remaining paper rolls. I got a hell of a good price on them from the publisher up in Havre. Newsprint! You'd think it was gold. It sure hasn't generated any lately.

(SONNY stares blankly at him.)

LIVINGSTON (cont.)
Oh, and the locksmith will be here at nine to change everything out, so never mind turning in your keys. Keep them as mementoes. Oh, and the office equipment liquidators will be here in the morning. Your desk will be worth much more to me unoccupied than occupied. Anyway, so much to do, so much to do. Well, goodbye, Sonny.

(LIVINGSTON begins to exit, then stops, as if remembering something. He goes back into the office, with SONNY watching him warily, and heads to where the dartboard/family photo hangs. He turns it around again, revealing his own face, then matches the image with a smarmy smile and departs, exiting the stage.)

SONNY
I was wrong. He's an unparalleled ghoul.

(SONNY stands, walks to the dartboard, pulls it off the wall and drops it to the ground. That seems to enervate him. He crosses back to the desk and engages the intercom.)

WOMAN'S VOICE
Yes, sir?

SONNY
Ginger, did he tell you what he just told me?

WOMAN'S VOICE
Yes, sir.

SONNY
Did he give you a check?

WOMAN'S VOICE
Yes, sir.

SONNY
No need to stick around, then. Go on home. Take good care, and thanks for
everything.

WOMAN'S VOICE
Thank you, sir.

*(SONNY disengages the intercom. He leans heavily on his two palms, bracing the desk.
He looks at the clock. He considers everything.)*

SONNY
(to himself, as if he doesn't believe it)
Twelve hours. Piece of cake.

(Blackout. End of scene.)

<blockquote>"Journalism can never be silent. That is its greatest virtue and its greatest fault."
Henry Anatole Grunwald</blockquote>

SCENE TWO

(The scene opens in SONNY's office, now occupied by SONNY and just one other person, a woman in her mid to late twenties. This is RANDI HUTCH, the chief reporter for the Sun. SONNY stands opposite her, behind his desk.)

SONNY
Where's everybody else?

RANDI
All four of us?

SONNY
Randi, come on. Where are they?

RANDI
Bruce unloads jets up at the airport every morning, remember? Tina is on vacation. Well, staycation. Her mom is in town, I think. Rex has been sick since Wednesday. Fourteen sick days this year, Sonny, if you're counting. I'm not counting. Why should I count? It's not my job.

SONNY
I should have fired his ass a long time ago.

RANDI
Knock, knock.

SONNY
(amused)
Who's there?

RANDI
Rex Wright.

SONNY
Rex Wright who? Or is it whom? Never did figure that one out.

RANDI
Sonny…

SONNY
Rex Wright who?

RANDI
Rex Wrights, but not too damn often if you're reading the *Sun*.

(The lame joke breaks them both up in laughter. SONNY gathers himself and effects a more somber posture.)

SONNY
Just you and me, then. I had a speech. I think I'll scrap it.

RANDI
Good idea. Better that way.

(SONNY fishes an envelope from the stack LIVINGSTON gave him and tosses it across the desk to RANDI, who catches it.)

SONNY
Open it and take a look.

(RANDI does as she's told. Her eyes go wide when she sees the contents.)

RANDI
Twenty-five thousand dollars.

SONNY
And not a cent more, ever. Livingston's shutting us down.

RANDI
(shocked)
When?

SONNY
Today.

RANDI
(on the verge of breaking)
Oh, Sonny.

SONNY
No, no, none of that. We have a paper to put out. Livingston wants a happy horseshit "thanks for the memories" sack of treacle out on front lawns in the morning, so let's get going.

RANDI
And you're going to do that?

SONNY
I don't see where I have much of a choice. So call the others, would you, and break it to them? Tell them to get their asses down here if they want to commit one last act of journalism before they're forced to go out and get real jobs. Tell them to come collect their checks, anyway. I really don't care if they work or not.

RANDI
And then?

SONNY
And then write something up, some kind of a goodbye. Tell people what you did for them. Tell them your favorite stories. Tell them whatever. We'll push it out and be done. You, me, whoever else wants to be a part of it, then we'll slap some wire copy around it, and that'll be that. Hands clean.

RANDI
No. I'm not going to do that.

SONNY
OK.

RANDI
I'd rather just go home, Sonny, than write a bunch of crap like that. That's an insult on top of the injury.

SONNY
If you say so. So go, then. I'll do it alone.

RANDI
Fine.

(RANDI turns on her heel and exits the office through the door. When she's offstage, SONNY collapses into his chair and starts moving the papers on his desk around, clearly lost about where to start amid the end of things. When he looks up, RANDI is standing inside the doorway, clearly angry.)

SONNY
What?

RANDI
I can't believe you're just going to roll over and die like this. What has happened to you?

(SONNY brushes a pile of papers from his desk in frustration.)

SONNY
Don't give me that crap.

RANDI
(feigning being impressed)
Oh, look, he lives.

SONNY
Goddammit, you've been here these last few years. Staff of thirty becomes a staff of twenty becomes a staff of ten becomes a staff of five. Well, the regression is over now. Livingston dropped the bomb. What am I supposed to fight for?

RANDI

The truth, dammit! What you've always fought for. The reason I came here, the reason I stayed, the reason I want to be done with my head high. We're not finished yet, Sonny. Don't let that go just because Livingston Fucking Sloane came in here and swung his dick around. You know what I'm talking about.

SONNY

Yeah, I know, and we're too late. We tried. We didn't make it. The hourglass is almost out of sand.

RANDI

So you're giving up?

SONNY

I am acknowledging reality.

RANDI

By giving up.

SONNY

(shaking his head)
Whatever you say.

RANDI

It's not what I'm saying. It's what you're doing. Or not.

(SONNY walks over to her, staring, silently imploring, ultimately saying nothing, because there is nothing to say. He turns away from RANDI and walks back to his desk. RANDI scampers out again. SONNY stops. His shoulders slump. He hangs his head. Then, in an instant, he's charged through with electricity and runs offstage, shouting.)

SONNY

Randi! Randi, wait!

(Blackout. End of scene.)

*"Journalism is printing what someone else does not want printed.
Everything else is public relations."*
George Orwell

SCENE THREE

(The scene opens with RANDI in SONNY's chair, her back to the office door as she types away at the computer terminal, which is the size and weight of a boulder. There is a knock at the glass office door and a grunt in return from RANDI, who is unmoved from her work. The man at the door, DEXTER COLLINS, prepares to knock again, almost puts his knuckles against the glass, then reconsiders and comes in.)

RANDI
(bearing down hard on her work)
Sit down. Don't say a word.

(DEXTER sits in one of the chairs fronting the desk. He's a large, muscular man, clearly uncomfortable with the fit he finds in it.)

DEXTER
Yes, ma'am.

(RANDI, without turning around, tersely holds up a hand like a stop sign.)

RANDI
I said…

(DEXTER *pulls pinched-together fingers across his lips like a zipper and makes like he's turning a key in a lock at the other side. RANDI winds up her burst of typing industry with a flourish, then spins around in the chair to get a look at the visitor.*)

RANDI
Who're you?

DEXTER
Dexter Collins, ma'am.

RANDI
Who is that?

DEXTER
Who is he.

RANDI
That's what I said.

DEXTER
No, I mean—

RANDI
If you don't know who you are, how are you going to tell me who you are, and how are we subsequently going to move this along, Dexter?

DEXTER
No, ma'am, I'm saying—

RANDI
Don't call me *ma'am*. It's patronizing.

DEXTER
OK, ma'am.

(*RANDI shoots him a withering look.*)

DEXTER (cont.)
OK.

RANDI
Thank you. Now, who're you?

DEXTER
(*standing up and offering a handshake*)
Dexter Collins.

RANDI
(*ignoring the offer*)
I think we've already been here.

DEXTER
Yes, and I was trying to tell you, you asked "who is that?" and I was trying to tell you I'm not a "that." I'm not a demonstrative pronoun. Proper style, I believe, is to say "who is he?" That's all I was saying.

(*RANDI's eyes narrow on DEXTER.*)

RANDI
Are you a grammar cop, Dexter?

DEXTER
No.

RANDI
Good. We could drown half of them and still have too many.

DEXTER
I was trying to show off and make a good impression.

RANDI
Oh, it totally didn't work.

DEXTER
I'm sorry.

RANDI
Anyway, what do you want?

DEXTER
I'm looking for Sonny Sturgis.

RANDI
He's not here.

DEXTER
I had begun to suspect not. When do you expect him?

RANDI
I don't.

DEXTER
Pardon?

RANDI
That is, I don't have expectations with regard to Sonny's appearance here or anywhere else. Wherever he is, that's where he needs to be. Whenever he comes back, that's when he's due here.

DEXTER
I see. Can I wait for him?

RANDI
Shouldn't that be "*may* I wait for him"?

DEXTER
Yes. Sorry.

RANDI
It's not like you, Dexter, to be so stylistically sloppy.

DEXTER
You're right. I'm sorry.

RANDI
Dexter?

DEXTER
Ma'am?

(He scrambles, having offended her again.)

DEXTER (cont.)
Yes? What?

RANDI
I'm just fucking with you.

DEXTER
(relieved)
OK. So can I—may I—wait?

RANDI
Can you, will you, do so quietly? I have a lot of work to do, as you can see, and I can't just jabber away the day with you.

DEXTER
I can. I will.

RANDI
Be my guest, then.

(RANDI bids DEXTER sit down, which he does, as uncomfortably as before. RANDI goes back to typing. DEXTER leans across the table, trying to get a look at its contents, craning his neck to look at papers at various angles. RANDI stops typing and turns around, and he rockets back into his seat, chastened.)

RANDI
Dexter Collins. Why do I know that name?

DEXTER
Do you like football?

RANDI
A foul, stupid sport designed to entertain morons.

DEXTER
So that's a no.

RANDI
I'm busy, Dexter. Sit still and be quiet, please.

(RANDI turns back to the computer, punches a few keys, then spins around again.)

RANDI
Why do you want to see Sonny?

DEXTER
Respectfully, ma'am—I'm sorry, Missus…

RANDI
Hutch. Randi Hutch. *Miss*. But spare me the honorifics.

DEXTER
(standing, almost reverent)
Randi Hutch!

RANDI
That's what I said.

DEXTER
I read your investigation last year, the one about the police union laundering money. Fantastic stuff. Really. Just top-notch. You're a role model.

RANDI
Oh my god.

DEXTER
What?

RANDI
You.

DEXTER
(looking himself over, checking his fly, touching his nose)
What?

RANDI
You want a job.

DEXTER
(relaxing)
Well, yeah, I guess…

(RANDI holds up a hand, stopping him. DEXTER sits down again.)

RANDI
It's better that you talk to Sonny.

(SONNY walks in. When he speaks, he startles RANDI and DEXTER.)

SONNY
Talk to me about what?

(He notes the presence of DEXTER, who stands up and turns to him.)

SONNY (cont.)
Who're you?

(RANDI turns off the computer she's working on, grabs an armful of papers from the desk, and beats a hasty exit.)

RANDI
I've already seen this part of the movie.

(RANDI brushes by them both, skirting a mild attempt by SONNY to stop her, and exits the stage. SONNY redirects his attention to DEXTER.)

SONNY
Who're you?

DEXTER
You don't remember me?

SONNY
Look, you're in my office.

DEXTER
Yes, I am.

(SONNY moves around DEXTER and reclaims his desk. He sits down. With exaggerated emphasis, he signals DEXTER to do the same.)

SONNY
Just so we're clear, in my office, I ask the questions, OK? You supply the answers to those questions, OK?

DEXTER
OK.

SONNY
Who are you?

DEXTER
Dexter Collins.

SONNY
The All-America safety?

DEXTER
Yes, sir.

SONNY
For the Griz?

DEXTER
(amused)
Yes, sir.

SONNY
Why?

DEXTER
Eleven interceptions last season. Twenty-one for my career. They really didn't
have a choice.

SONNY
No, why are you here?

DEXTER
You really don't remember.

SONNY
Listen, Dexter Collins…

DEXTER
That was a declarative sentence, not a question. You really don't.

SONNY
(exasperated)
I really don't.

DEXTER
Missoula, last year. You spoke to my journalism class. You got into a bit of an argument with my professor, who asked you what advice you'd give to students who aspired to management careers in journalism. Do you remember that?

SONNY
Vaguely. Sort of.

DEXTER
You said, "Suck on some cyanide now and do the world a favor."

SONNY
Ah, yes. I stand by that.

DEXTER
I took note of you then. I took further note of you that night at the Top Hat, after you invited some of us out for a drink. Remember now?

SONNY
Not so much. Can't say a night at the Top Hat is exactly a rarity when I'm in Missoula.

DEXTER
Well, I remember. Not the first time I ever saw a man get drunk, but it was the first time I ever saw a drunk man recite Shakespeare…

SONNY
Oh, god.

DEXTER
…while standing on the bar…

SONNY
Oh, god.

DEXTER
…after telling the band that their instruments, and this is a direct quote, "bray like dying farm animals."

SONNY
Here's another direct quote: "Oh, god."

DEXTER

It's coming back to you.

SONNY

I wish it weren't.

DEXTER

Well, anyway, a few of us made sure you got to the Holiday Inn safely. Me, I went home and looked up the Shakespeare bit—*Romeo and Juliet*, right?—and read it and reread it until I knew all the words. I figured if it could come out clean from your memory after a night of heavy booze, it must mean something mighty important.

(At this, SONNY, clearly ashamed, stands up, catching DEXTER by surprise. He intones the next bit.)

SONNY

Give me my Romeo; and, when he shall die, / Take him and cut him out in little stars, / And he will make the face of heaven so fine / That all the world will be in love with night / And pay no worship to the garish sun.

DEXTER

(as if awestruck)
That's it.

SONNY

Wasn't the first time I'd recited it. Might be the last, though. I don't believe it the way I once did.

DEXTER

What does it mean?

SONNY

It's us. It's what we do here. We're in love with night, when all our daily work comes together, and if we do that work well—and it's only about the most important work there is, which is why I chewed on your professor's ass so hard, for being so reductive as to talk about careers when it's goddamn democracy on the line—we make the face of heaven so fine with the difference it makes. I figure if you need a mission statement, you can do a hell of a lot worse than filching one off good ol' Billy Shakes.

DEXTER
(reverently)
It's beautiful.

SONNY
It's about the most beautiful thing ever committed to parchment. You've got
a good ear, Dexter.

(DEXTER preens under the praise.)

SONNY (cont.)
Now…why're you here?

DEXTER
I need a job.

SONNY
Oh.

DEXTER
You told us that night, you said—

SONNY
I said, "After you graduate, look me up. I need good young reporters."

DEXTER
That's what you said.

SONNY
I know. That's what I always say.

DEXTER
So here I am.

SONNY
Jesus, Dexter. Why'd you have to be the first one to take me up on it?

DEXTER
I'm a good young reporter, and I need a job.

SONNY
I see.

DEXTER
You offered. Shouldn't have done that if you didn't want to see me again.

SONNY
Dexter, I don't remember seeing you the first time.

DEXTER
Nonetheless.

SONNY
And I don't have a job for you.

(RANDI comes sweeping into the office, clutching a sheath of papers. The next series of lines is a rapid-fire back and forth between RANDI and SONNY as DEXTER looks on, increasingly shrinking and overwhelmed.)

RANDI
Did you tell him we don't have a job for him?

SONNY
I was just getting to that.

RANDI
Did you tell him why?

SONNY
I hadn't gotten to that yet.

RANDI
Did you tell him that Livingston Sloane is a corrupt, consumptive son of a bitch?

SONNY
It didn't seem germane to the topic at hand.

RANDI
Did you tell him we're being shut down?

SONNY
No.

RANDI
Did you tell him we're all out on our ass tonight?

SONNY
I didn't—

RANDI
Did you tell him everything is hopeless but we're going to try anyway?

SONNY
It would lack context to say that.

RANDI
Did you tell him he's better off going back to first base?

SONNY
Huh?

(*SONNY looks helplessly at them both, shrugging.*)

RANDI
Sonny, did you tell him *anything*?

DEXTER
(*regaining himself*)
I was a football player.

RANDI and SONNY
(*simultaneously*)
Huh?

DEXTER
First base, that's not football, it's…Never mind.

RANDI
Football. Stupid sport for people born without brain stems.

SONNY
Enough!

(*SONNY wanders around the office, trying to get his bearings, while RANDI and DEXTER hang back, cowed by his outburst. Finally, he faces them.*)

SONNY

Thank you, Randi, for bringing our guest up to speed in your inimitable way. Tonight, when you're done being a reporter, you should consider a second career as a badger. Dexter, I do not have a job for you, but I admire your grit and your initiative and your good humor, and if you're game, I think we can put a little money in your pocket and further your journalism education in a most unconventional way that might, if we're lucky, not land us all in jail.

RANDI

Sonny, what are you—

SONNY

(cutting her off)
Are you game, Dexter?

DEXTER

Do I have to do anything illegal?

SONNY

Define *illegal.*

DEXTER

My mother, she'd never get over it if I did anything illegal.

SONNY

I don't want to lie to you, Dexter. So let me say this: There's a chance that something we do tonight—even several somethings—could be construed as illegal by someone with a vested interest in being parsimonious about illegality. I'm no moral relativist, but I dare say that many—indeed, most—of the laws written in this country exist as a sort of toggle switch. They restrain or define one thing or one set of people, and on the flip side they abet or enable something else or someone else. Folks like us, Dexter, we are the restrained. We are the defined. And those who are in the other group run roughshod over us every single day of our existence. Tonight, for one night, we're going to level the field.

So, yes, you might do something illegal. But your mother, if she's anything like her son, will be proud of you for doing it. You'll be proud of you. Your kids, should you ever have any, will be proud of you. *I* will be proud of you. So I ask again: Are you game?

DEXTER
Yes, sir. You bet I am.

SONNY
Good.

RANDI
Goddammit, Sonny, this is why I love you.

SONNY
(gripping her neck affectionately)
OK, here's the plan. Randi has been closing in on an expose of the mayor. Kickbacks, influence peddling, poor comportment with city employees. A real horse's ass, is what I'm saying, and exactly the kind of person we don't need in positions of public trust, never mind that we seem to be enduring a ceaseless stream of them. The problem, the first problem—

RANDI
Livingston Sloane.

DEXTER
The owner of the paper.

SONNY
No. I mean, yes. But I mean, no, that's not the first problem.

RANDI
Livingston Sloane will never let us print that story.

DEXTER
Why not?

(RANDI begins to speak, but SONNY cuts her off.)

SONNY
The first problem is that we don't have the story nailed down, and we're almost out of time. Nine hours, Randi. Nine. So you'd better get moving.

RANDI
Piece of cake.

(RANDI dashes offstage.)

DEXTER
What's the second problem?

SONNY
Randi's right. Livingston Sloane will never let us print that story.

DEXTER
Why not?

SONNY
Because the mayor, Dillon Sloane, is his brother. And because Livingston Sloane is a corrupt, consumptive son of a bitch.

DEXTER
So what are you gonna do?

SONNY
I'm still figuring that out.

DEXTER
So what do you need me to do?

SONNY
I'm still figuring that out, too. But I promise you this: It's gonna be fun. You're doing the right thing, Dexter.

(Blackout. End of scene.)

"Th newspaper does ivrything f'r us. It runs th' polis foorce an' th' banks, commands th' milishy, controls th' ligislachure, baptizes th' young, marries th' foolish, comforts th' afflicted, afflicts th' comfortable, buries th' dead an' roasts thim aftherward."
Finley Peter Dunne

ACT TWO

SCENE FOUR

(The scene opens with DEXTER alone at the table in SONNY's office, reading intently from large, bound books of previous newspapers. Occasionally, DEXTER jots down a note on a yellow legal pad, then goes back to his reading. A woman, ANNA STURGIS, comes to the office door and tentatively peeks in. DEXTER spots and greets her.)

DEXTER
Hi.

(ANNA, with some hesitation, moves fully into the office.)

ANNA
Hi. Who're you?

DEXTER
I need a name tag. They should have given me a name tag.

ANNA
Pardon?

DEXTER
I'm Dexter. I'm new.

ANNA
Hi, Dexter. Where's Sonny?

DEXTER
Out.

ANNA
Obviously.

DEXTER
I don't know where. But he should be back soon. He has a lot to do.

ANNA
OK if I wait?

DEXTER
Sure. Have a seat.

(*DEXTER scooches over a bit, moving the book of old newspapers to give ANNA some room at the table. ANNA sits down, a bit warily, and DEXTER smiles awkwardly, then returns to his work. After a brief silence, ANNA speaks.*)

ANNA
What are you doing?

DEXTER
(*putting his pencil down and shoving the book away*)
I am taking a crash course in the *Sun*'s recent journalistic history.

ANNA
I see.

DEXTER
That is, Sonny told me to read three months' worth of papers and write down every headline I think sucks—pardon my language, ma'am, but that's what he said—and every story that I think has a fundamental problem in its reporting. He's testing me.

ANNA
That sounds like something he would do.

DEXTER
He's a brilliant guy.

ANNA
How long have you worked here, Dexter?

DEXTER
Started today. Why?

ANNA
Give yourself some time on the brilliance bit, OK? Sonny is just a guy.

(DEXTER looks at her oddly, as if wondering where the low-key invective is coming from. After a few seconds, realization dawns on his face.)

DEXTER
(pointing at ANNA)
I know you.

ANNA
You do?

(DEXTER stands up and goes to the other side of the office, where he picks up the dartboard/family portrait that SONNY threw down earlier. He shows it to her.)

DEXTER
This is you, yes?

ANNA
(in wonderment)
Yes. A long time ago.

DEXTER
Looks like you. How long ago?

ANNA
(sighing)
Lifetimes.

(DEXTER now points at the face of the little boy in the picture.)

DEXTER
And who's this?

ANNA
(quietly)
Matthew.

DEXTER
Very cute kid.

ANNA
(ever quieter)
Thank you.

(SONNY comes striding into the office, aggressiveness in his movements.)

SONNY
He's also a very dead kid, which she will go to every possible length not to tell you, because she would have to admit the truth and the circumstances of it to herself, and that, Dexter, is something Anna is loath to do, even though she knows—surely, she must know by now—that it's the only way through the hell she insists on living in.

(SONNY turns now to his wife.)

SONNY (cont.)
Hello, dear. What brings you downtown? It's the worst possible day for a visit.

ANNA
Dammit, Sonny.

DEXTER
Oh my god.

(SONNY pivots his attention back to DEXTER.)

SONNY
How goes your assignment?

DEXTER
Fi—it's fine.

SONNY
Good. I want you to set it aside. I have a more important task for you.

DEXTER
OK.

SONNY
I want you to go to the city offices. Third floor, finance department. I want you to ask to see Maxwell Duncan. When his secretary asks who you are—and she will—tell her you're a friend of his son's and he's expecting you. I want you to sit there until she lets you in to see him. I want you to sit there politely and smile, but make no small talk and utter not a word about who sent you, OK? When, at last, you lay eyes on Maxwell Duncan—who will be the most sniveling, sickly man you've ever seen in your life—I want you to say these words to him: "I'm here for the pumpkin." You got that?

DEXTER
City offices, third floor, finance, Maxwell Duncan, friend of his son's, on the downlow, here for the pumpkin.

SONNY
Precisely that. And here's the most important thing: You bring what he gives you back here to me. You don't say a word about this errand, you hear me? You bring it here, and you hand it to me and only me. Got that?

DEXTER
Got it. Where are the city offices?

(SONNY gives him a stare that could cut glass.)

DEXTER (cont.)
Never mind. I'll find them.

(DEXTER dashes out of the office. SONNY goes and sits behind his desk while ANNA remains seated at the table, a bit rattled by the gravity of seeing her husband in his element.)

SONNY
Really, Anna, it's just a terrible day.

ANNA
That's a thin excuse, Sonny. Every day is a terrible day for this, according to you, and yet here I am.

SONNY
Here you are.

ANNA
(removing an envelope from her purse)
I brought the papers, same as the last three times I've been here. It's everything we agreed to. Everything we've already divided. Really, Sonny, just a signature and I'll be gone, for good. You'll never see me again.

SONNY
In this town? Oh, I'll see you.

ANNA
You'll never intentionally see me again.

SONNY
And you think that's what I want?

(ANNA leaps to her feet and presses in on SONNY, who's taken aback.)

ANNA
I don't know what you want, which is the whole problem, which has been the whole problem for months now. Years now. You and I, we settled this thing between us. This is what we came up with, we had it drawn up legally, and now you won't sign the goddamn paperwork, Sonny! That is the entire issue, beginning, middle, and end. Will you please, please sign it now? Please?

(Wordlessly, SONNY signals for ANNA to lower the temperature, to sit down. After

some struggle against herself, she does.)

SONNY
(quietly)
What is the hurry? Why does it have to be divorce, right now, today?

ANNA
Not today. Yesterday. Last week. Last month. Last winter. Sonny, this has been coming for a long, long time.

SONNY
But divorce. Why? To what end? It's severed. We're severed, Anna. What's the point of the legalistics, unless you're planning to get…

(ANNA looks up, as if he has inadvertently tripped over the truth. SONNY recognizes this and stands, then comes around the desk and faces her.)

SONNY (cont.)
No, no, no, no, nononononono. No. Absolutely not. Get on with your life— that's your right, but not that way. And not with him.

ANNA
(standing)
Of all the monumental gall. Sonny, try to get this: You don't have the right of first refusal here. You don't get to vote on who I'm with or what I do or when I do it. Nobody, least of all me, gives a shit what you have to say about it.

SONNY
He's a bad man.

ANNA
(ferociously)
He loves me.

SONNY
(with equal ferocity)
I loved you.

(They both retreat from each other a bit, energy drained from the fervor of their exchange.)

ANNA
And there it is. Past tense.

SONNY
You lost interest in my present tense after we lost Matthew.

ANNA
No—

SONNY
You know you did.

ANNA
You weren't there. That night, when it happened. A thousand nights before. And after, when we were both hurting so bad and might have had a chance to pull each other through…

SONNY
After, I just had to find a way to stay alive. To forgive myself. To try to gain your forgiveness.

(ANNA moves up to SONNY, who flinches. She reaches for him. She pulls him into a hug.)

ANNA
I had nothing to forgive. But I could not find my way back to you, nor could I give you a way back to me. You act like I didn't try. I tried. I was the only one who tried.

SONNY
(disengaging)
You didn't.

ANNA
I did. But I can't anymore. I won't anymore.

SONNY
And there it is.

(SONNY steps back.)

SONNY (cont.)
You made me leave.

ANNA
I didn't want to. I had to.

SONNY
And now, now you're with…*him*? You're just going to go on with *him*?

ANNA
Sonny, don't.

SONNY
Our memories, our pain, our joys, which we sometimes had, our failures, our triumphs, they're going to live on in the background while you try it again with *him*?

ANNA
Sonny…

SONNY
Go home, Anna. I'm not signing shit.

ANNA
Sonny, please.

SONNY
(with all the ferocity he can muster)
Go home!

(ANNA at last scurries away, and she nearly collides with RANDI at the office door. The two women look each other over, with cordial smiles that are wary rather than warm. RANDI comes fully into the office. ANNA steps fully out, pauses a beat, then comes back in.)

ANNA
This is the last time, Sonny. I'd hoped we could avoid lawyers, but maybe we can't. I won't be back here. But I will get what I want, the hard way or the easier way.

(RANDI turns toward ANNA.)

RANDI
You won't be back here because—

SONNY
Shut up, Randi.

(He turns his attention to ANNA.)

SONNY (cont.)
Do what you must, all right?

(RANDI sits down in a huff. ANNA exits the stage. SONNY stares off after her.)

SONNY
Where do we stand?

RANDI
I have some of it. Not all.

SONNY
What's missing?

RANDI
The same stuff that's always been missing. The financials. The meat. The thing that lets us say, "We've got you now, motherfucker."

SONNY
We'll be OK.

RANDI
What does that—

SONNY
We'll be OK.

RANDI
What difference does it make if Livingston won't let the papers off the dock—

SONNY
Just keep working it and writing it and let me worry about that.

RANDI
Sonny, what in the hell—

SONNY
(*wheeling on her*)
Just get it done, OK?

RANDI
Jesus. OK. What's with you?

(*SONNY doesn't answer. He turns back to the door and looks at it, almost wistfully.*)

SONNY
I'll be right back. Get to work.

(*SONNY dashes out. RANDI, perturbed, sits down at his desk, turns on the computer, and waits for the screen to come up.*)

RANDI
Fucking ay, right? Why tell me? I'm only the reporter. Jesus, Sonny, I hope you know what you're into here.

(*Blackout. End of scene.*)

"Journalism will kill you, but it will keep you alive while you're at it."
Horace Greeley

SCENE FIVE

(The scene opens with RANDI at the computer behind SONNY's desk, alternately checking her paperwork and going back to the keyboard and typing. After a few moments, DEXTER, out of breath, barrels into the office.)

DEXTER
I've got—

(DEXTER stops short, seeing that SONNY isn't there. RANDI, annoyed, turns around in her chair.)

RANDI
You've got what?

DEXTER
Nothing.

RANDI
Oh, you're going to try that, huh?

DEXTER
Lunch.

RANDI
It's barely ten a.m.

DEXTER
Early lunch. Where's Sonny?

RANDI
Out. You fit lunch into that manila envelope, did you? Well, give it to me, then. I'm starving.

(RANDI points at what DEXTER carries under his arm. DEXTER flushes with shame at the feebleness of his excuse.)

RANDI (cont.)
Unsolicited advice, Dexter: Don't go into politics. You're a terrible liar.

DEXTER
(sitting at the table)
Will he be back soon?

RANDI
Dunno.

DEXTER
I'll wait.

RANDI
(pointing again)
Whatcha got there?

DEXTER
Something for Sonny.

RANDI
What is it?

DEXTER
I'd rather just give it to Sonny, OK?

RANDI
(tauntingly)
Deeeexteeeer…

DEXTER
Please. OK? You got me. It's not lunch. Just leave me alone, OK?

RANDI
(shrugging)
Fine. I must tell you, though, this is not a shimmering example of teamwork.

(DEXTER fumes at the jibe. RANDI eventually spins back around and returns to her work. DEXTER picks up the archival materials he was thumbing through earlier and looks at them listlessly, clearly not engaged by what he's reading. At last, he speaks.)

DEXTER
Can I ask you something?

(RANDI gruffly turns around in her chair.)

RANDI
Oh, so now you want something from me?

DEXTER
It's a simple yes or no. I didn't ask you anything open-ended, so no need for editorializing. Now, can I ask you something or not?

RANDI
Yes, you may.

DEXTER
What's the deal with Sonny and his wife?

RANDI
Oh, no.

DEXTER
What?

RANDI
That's not a question, Dexter. That's, like, twenty questions, a pop quiz, a personality profile, two FBI investigations, and a half-dozen confessionals.

DEXTER
Wow.

RANDI
I might be a tad hyperbolic.

DEXTER
As long as it's only a tad.

RANDI
They're divorcing.

DEXTER
I figured that part out.

RANDI
Sonny isn't happy about it.

DEXTER
That part, too. What happened to Matthew?

(The broaching of the name tumbles RANDI into a seeming sadness.)

RANDI
So much for yes-no questions, huh?

DEXTER
(pleading)
What?

(RANDI gets up and comes around the desk, sits next to DEXTER at the table, and commands his attention with her intensity.)

RANDI
He was hit by a car. Killed. A year and a half ago.

DEXTER
(shocked into deep sadness)
No.

RANDI
Sonny, he'll never get over it. Never. He went home that night to have din-

ner with Anna and Matthew. Election night. Busy night here, but he went home and had dinner, tried to make it as normal as he could, this being a decidedly abnormal job and all. They ate, they talked, you know, family stuff, and I guess Sonny scolded Matthew about something, and the kid took off, grabbed his skateboard, tore out of there, whipping away down the street. Sonny came back to the office. Never saw his son again. Got the call while we're standing there monitoring election returns. He goes ghost-white. He left. He—the guy he was—never came back. We never saw him again, in the way he was before it happened. The same man showed up every day after they buried Matthew, but he's a different guy.

DEXTER
Oh my god.

RANDI
Anna told me what had happened at the house, by the way. Sonny, he…well, he's just different now, that's all. There's a sadness within him that just…I don't know. He's lost inside it.

DEXTER
Can't blame him.

RANDI
I don't. How could I? I'm in love with him.

DEXTER
(taken aback)
Huh?

RANDI
A condition that far predates what happened to Matthew, I should add. And a condition of which Sonny is entirely unaware. And you would be, too, if I hadn't just told you, for whatever damn reason I chose to do that. So exercise some discretion, would you, please?

(DEXTER stands up, gobsmacked. He takes a few steps away from RANDI.)

DEXTER
You're in love with him?

RANDI
Jesus, Dexter, pull yourself together. It's not Hallmark love. It's deeper than

that and purer than that. Sonny Sturgis is the most extraordinarily brilliant man I have ever met, with a mind that can bounce from economics to geo-politics to public lands to Montana high school sports to fine art to Shake-speare…

DEXTER
He loves Shakespeare.

RANDI
So you know what I'm talking about. I don't want to have sex with him, Dexter.

(RANDI pauses, as if considering the prospect for the first time.)

RANDI (cont.)
Although I guess I probably would, in the vanishingly unlikely case that were a situation we found ourselves in. I want to bear his brilliance. That's what I'm saying. I want to help him give birth to a thousand acts of righteous journalism. I want to see his eyes light up, I want him to climb up on a desk, and I want him to bellow, "Tonight, we put out the best fucking paper in the country. In the world!" The way he used to. The way he hasn't done since he lost his boy. The way he won't, not ever again, it looks like, thanks to Living-ston Sloane.

(DEXTER again sits down with her.)

DEXTER
I don't think I've ever felt that way about anyone.

RANDI
Well, consider yourself lucky. It's a terrible affliction.

DEXTER
Maybe you're wrong. Maybe he will do that again, one more time. Maybe tonight.

RANDI
No.

DEXTER
Maybe.

RANDI
One, we don't have the story, and the clock is running out. Two, even if we had the story, Livingston would never let it get off the loading dock. This is the end, Dexter. I wish you could have seen the beginning. Or even the middle.

DEXTER
So what are we doing here, then? Spinning our wheels?

RANDI
I am seeing this through to the end, waiting to see what Sonny's going to do, bracing myself for the high likelihood that he isn't going to do anything except go out with a whimper, and hoping I can survive the witnessing of that. You are working for one day at your first journalism job, and it'll be your last if luck is at all on your side.

DEXTER
And Sonny?

RANDI
Sonny doesn't know what else to do.

(RANDI delivers the line as SONNY comes into the office.)

SONNY
What else should I do?

(Startled, RANDI scurries back to the computer and begins typing. DEXTER fidgets, as if wondering how much SONNY has heard. SONNY, arms crossed on his chest, observes them bemusedly.)

SONNY (cont.)
I let you use my computer because I thought you'd be working.

RANDI
I am working.

SONNY
(dismissively)
Yeah, you're working.

RANDI
You'd better be nice to me, Sonny. I'm all you have left.

SONNY
(waving toward DEXTER)
Not true. I have our newest recruit.

RANDI
Dexter and me, then. Or is it Dexter and I? I always get that one wrong…

DEXTER
Colloquially, you're fine.

SONNY
Jesus.

RANDI
Point is, the others came in and picked up their checks while you and Dexter were out. This is the dream team, right here in this room. So don't be too much of a dick, OK?

SONNY
(amused)
OK. Do you have it?

RANDI
Not yet.

SONNY
Are you gonna have it?

RANDI
(facing him)
Is it gonna matter?

SONNY
Yes, it is.

RANDI
Then yes, I will.

SONNY
Good.

(SONNY turns to DEXTER.)

SONNY (cont.)
Do you have it?

DEXTER
(waving the manila envelope)
I have it.

RANDI
What is it?

SONNY
Never mind.

RANDI
It's the pumpkin, isn't it?

SONNY
Yes, yes, it's the pumpkin.

RANDI
(explosively)
Goddammit, no. I told you. No.

DEXTER
See, this is where I'd like to ask…

RANDI and SONNY
(simultaneously)
Shut up, Dexter.

(DEXTER shrinks.)

RANDI
(now focused entirely on SONNY)
I will not get the story this way. I won't. It's my story, Sonny, not yours. It's my story to get my way.

SONNY
(*also explosive*)
It's not a story at all yet, is it? But this will make it one if we need it. *If*, Randi.
You can ensure that we don't need it, of course, but you haven't done that
yet, and we're running out of time.

RANDI
Nope. No way.

DEXTER
Hey, dream team? A little communication, please?

(*RANDI and SONNY look menacingly at each other, then unclench just a bit.
SONNY waves at her to get back to work.*)

SONNY
Sorry, Dex. You've wandered into a pile of shit here.

(*SONNY sits down with DEXTER, then calls out to RANDI, whose back is to them.*)

SONNY (cont.)
Chime in whenever you're so compelled.

RANDI
Oh, you know I will.

SONNY
Anyway, you met Max Duncan, the man with eternal post-nasal drip. He was
my college roommate. … Where are you from, Dexter?

DEXTER
Massachusetts.

RANDI
(*spinning in the chair*)
Really?

DEXTER
Yeah.

RANDI
How'd you manage Massachusetts to Montana?

DEXTER
(shrugging)
Football scholarship. Good journalism school. Didn't have many competing
offers.

(DEXTER redirects to SONNY.)

DEXTER (cont.)
You were saying?

RANDI
(spinning back to the computer)
Football. Inexplicable sport for people who think with their dicks because
they haven't got any brains.

SONNY
Anyway, it's as I was saying: Inverse to Massachusetts, Montana is a big state
for geography, Dexter, but remarkably puny when it comes to personal con-
nections. So imagine this: You're a kid from Melstone, a little dot on the
Montana map, and you go off to Bozeman for college and think you're making some huge move, then it turns out your freshman roomie is from Ingo-
mar, an even tinier dot, and your parents have known his parents for decades,
and your mom squeals and says, "Well, isn't it just a small world?" Yeah, it
is. Too goddamn small, for my money. Because you're gonna be seeing Max
Duncan for the rest of your stinking life.

But it's not all bad, because Max Duncan becomes the reason you know
some of the things you know about Mayor Sloane. The city contracts for his
buddies. The shell companies that somehow end up dumping city monies
directly into the mayor's pockets. The HR complaints about his wandering
hands, reports that end up going nowhere, and isn't that strange? How he not
so subtly lets it be known that defying him will put you in the crosshairs of
his litigious brother Livingston, who just happens to be the owner and chief
asshole of this soon-to-be-former daily rag.

RANDI
(turning around again)
Of course, none of this is on the record. Sonny hears this stuff over beers.
Small talk. Scuttlebutt. Nothing on paper. Nothing on the record. But it's
good to know, anyway, because we can start to piece it together. Try to, anyway. A lot of big stories are that way. There's what you know, and what you
can print, and the trick is getting those two things to meet in the middle.

SONNY
Which is what we've been doing. But the tracks are old, some of them, and people are scared to go on the record, and the paper trail is thin to nonexistent.

DEXTER
Duncan seemed scared, handing me that envelope.

SONNY
He should be, both for his professional skin and for the things I know that he'd prefer I didn't. I called in a favor. A big one. He owes me.

DEXTER
Which is?

SONNY
End of the line, Dexter. Sorry.

RANDI
It's not just the favor, though. It's the motivation.

SONNY
End of the line, I said.

RANDI
No. Fuck no. I'm saying it.

SONNY
Fine.

DEXTER
What?

RANDI
I don't trust why Sonny called in the favor. And that's heartbreaking because I trust Sonny more than anyone. But not on this.

SONNY
It's not heartbreaking. It's bullshit.

RANDI
It's reality.

DEXTER
Why don't you trust him?

RANDI
(to SONNY)
You or me, boss? Probably better coming from you.

SONNY
Just tell him.

RANDI
Mayor Sloane is boning Sonny's wife.

SONNY
(wincing)
Jesus. A little grace, please.

DEXTER
Really?

SONNY
Yeah, really. Come on, Dexter, try not to sound so titillated.

RANDI
Yeah. So, look, the mayor is a bad dude, and he deserves whatever fallout comes from his malfeasance and creepiness, but it's the fact that he's dating Anna that finally got Sonny really moving on this story, and that's the wrong goddamn reason to develop some alacrity.

SONNY
I didn't think we could get it before!

RANDI
You didn't want to get it before, because you've been sleepwalking for the better part of two years now, and you won't admit it. But I did want it, and I do want it, and I'm gonna get it. Without whatever you held over Max to prompt him to give up the goods.

(SONNY shoots to his feet.)

SONNY
Fine! Stop talking about it and fucking do it, then.

RANDI
I will. Not that it matters. Livingston will never let it happen.

SONNY
Livingston's apple cart is about to be turned over.

RANDI
What does that mean?

SONNY
Just do your job and let me do mine, OK? Come on, Dexter.

DEXTER
Where are we going?

SONNY
I'll tell you when we get there.

DEXTER
What are we gonna do?

SONNY
Some of those illegal things we talked about before.

(SONNY and DEXTER exit. RANDI stands as they leave.)

RANDI
Holy shit.

(Blackout. End of scene. Intermission.)

"The man who reads nothing at all is better educated than the man who reads nothing but newspapers."
Thomas Jefferson

SCENE SIX

(The scene opens with SONNY and DEXTER coming into SONNY's office looking disheveled: shirttails out, grease stains on their clothes, splashes of paint on their cheeks. SONNY wears heavy work gloves, which he casts off after sitting down at his desk. DEXTER, taking his own seat at the table, follows suit with his gloves.)

SONNY
I wasn't sure what to make of you this morning, Dex, but thanks. I truly couldn't have done that without you.

DEXTER
Without my muscle, you mean.

SONNY
Yes, that. But mostly your willingness. Your trust.

DEXTER
I feel sick to my stomach.

SONNY
I understand.

(*SONNY begins rooting through his desk drawers.*)

SONNY (cont.)
I think I have some Pepto around here somewhere.

DEXTER
I'll be OK.

SONNY
You sure?

(*DEXTER nods. He sets his head into his hands, as if waiting for a wave of nausea to pass, before he looks up again.*)

DEXTER
The thing is, I don't understand what we just did.

SONNY
You ever hear of asymmetrical warfare, Dexter?

DEXTER
I think so.

SONNY
Insurgencies, counterinsurgencies, guerrilla tactics. Hell, the entire founding of this republic, right? You have a regular army, the British, massive and indomitable, lining up in proper columns and going about its business in established ways. What's a ragtag group of freedom fighters to do? Hang out in trees. Attack from odd angles. Get the big boys off their footing, then take them down.

DEXTER
Professor Florio always told us that war imagery was hackneyed writing and poor journalism.

SONNY
(*amused but also exasperated*)
OK, OK, fine. She's right, by the way. Let's try this: Remember when you guys beat North Dakota State a couple of years back?

DEXTER
Sure. How could I forget?

SONNY
Your interception sealed it, right?

DEXTER
Yes, sir.

SONNY
What happened there?

DEXTER
I beat their guy to the ball.

SONNY
But what *happened?*

DEXTER
Coach had us in a zone shell, to keep all the action in front of us and protect our lead. But their tight end had a tell. When he'd line up and the fingers on his free hand would twitch, I knew he'd be going out rather than blocking down. They overloaded the other side, and we shifted that way. I had a feeling he'd be going the other way on a short route. So I broke from the shell at the snap.

SONNY
This was just a feeling you had?

DEXTER
More than a feeling. I had observational intel.

SONNY
And you did something unpredictable, that wasn't part of the defense you were in. Something that might have been disastrous if you were wrong.

DEXTER
Yes, sir. But I was right.

SONNY
Asymmetrical warfare! Er, football-fare! Get it?

DEXTER
I get the concept. I just don't see the connection here. If I have a newspaper to put out, newsprint is something I need. A press to put it on is something I need. What am I missing?

SONNY
Certainly not a commitment to conventional thinking.

DEXTER
Huh?

SONNY
You're absolutely right, Dexter. But Randi is right, too. Livingston will never let us publish anything worth the paper it's printed on. We've simply cleared the decks of that possibility.

DEXTER
So what do we do with our story?

SONNY
Do we have a story?

DEXTER
We'll have one when Randi gets it, which she will.

SONNY
You sure?

DEXTER
Yes, sir. She will. I trust her.

SONNY
Good. So do I.

DEXTER
So what do we do?

SONNY
I don't have that part totally figured out yet.

DEXTER
Oh, shit. You're being—

SONNY
Asymmetrical?

DEXTER
Irresponsible. Foolish.

SONNY
(chuckling)
Agreed.

(SONNY stands and comes around the desk, fishing his wallet from his back pocket. He opens it, removes a check, and hands it to DEXTER.)

SONNY
For you. For a day of services rendered. Thank you, Dexter.

(DEXTER unfurls the check and registers surprise at what he sees.)

DEXTER
Ten thousand dollars.

SONNY
I raided Livingston's retirement gift to me. Sorry I couldn't give you the gold watch. There wasn't one.

DEXTER
I can't take this.

SONNY
You'd better. Nobody can be sure how this is all going to look in a few hours. And these might be the only journalism dollars you ever see in your whole life.

DEXTER
I've considered that.

SONNY
I'm sorry. You were born too late. I wish you'd come to me ten years ago. We'd have done some great stuff together.

DEXTER
We still might.

SONNY
(surprised and pleased)
We might at that.

(SONNY goes back to his chair and lands heavily in it.)

SONNY (cont.)
OK, my young protégé, we have earned a ten-minute break. Ask me anything. Assume we'd have had a year or two together before some bigger outlet came along that could throw you more money and stature. Let's compress those years into our day together.

DEXTER
Anything?

SONNY
Anything at all.

DEXTER
OK. What's it like to win a Pulitzer Prize?

SONNY
That's the best you've got?

DEXTER
That's the *first* I've got.

SONNY
(exhaling)
Fine. I'm afraid I won't be particularly dazzling in my articulation. I mean, it's the biggest phone call you'll ever get in your career, and the immensity of that moment is hard to prepare for. I knew it was a possibility, but it wasn't something I allowed myself to think about, so I didn't gird up for it. You get the call, they tell you that you've won, and the room, it starts spinning.

DEXTER
I can only imagine.

SONNY
The money, it's surprisingly paltry. Ten grand back then.

SONNY (cont.)
Yeah. I used it to feather the newsroom budget so I didn't have to lay anyone off that year. Not near enough to keep everybody forever, though.

There are ancillary benefits, I guess. It's been a long time since I've bought my own drink unless I insist. Plenty of invitations to come speak, sometimes for a small stipend, and sometimes for a really big one. There's a permanence to it. That's the big thing. You realize pretty quickly that it will always be a part of how you're introduced. It'll be the first line in your obituary. That's something, I guess.

DEXTER
But how did it *feel?*

SONNY
Honestly?

DEXTER
Of course honestly. It's too early for us to start lying to each other.

SONNY
(laughing)
You're a funny guy, Dexter. It feels like the worst kind of impostor syndrome. We celebrated the win, of course—god, yes, we did, and I got about as drunk as I ever have—but at some point you have to reckon with why it happened at all. I won for breaking news, Dexter, and that usually means that your award-winning work rides on the back of some truly shitty circumstance for someone else. So, in a sense that you can never escape, you get lucky because someone else gets devastated. Or thirteen someones, multiplied across everyone who knows and loves them. Thirteen kids, dead on a burning bus on a field trip to a battlefield. That happened, and I won a Pulitzer. You think I'm happy with that bargain?

DEXTER
(solemnly)
No, sir.

SONNY
I tried to make my peace with it, but I'm not sure I ever got there. I used to say impotent things like "I'd trade it all for those kids to be back with their

mommies and daddies," thinking, you know, it sounds right and sounds respectful but not really understanding how that feels on the other side, to be the ones missing those kids, having nothing to show for what happened to them except heartache that can't be mended. And then I found out.

DEXTER
Matthew.

SONNY
Yes. My fated son.

(SONNY turns in his chair, away from DEXTER, who fidgets with the old newspapers on the table in front of him, clearly affected by the exchange. After a few beats, RANDI barrels into the office, out of breath, jerking them back to attention.)

RANDI
I got it.

(SONNY and DEXTER go quickly to their feet, and RANDI gets her first good look at them.)

RANDI (cont.)
What the hell happened to you guys?

SONNY
You got it? The whole smash?

RANDI
On the record, in document form. I got it. Copies of the HR reports that were buried. Got those, too.

SONNY
Holy shit! How?

RANDI
I'll tell you as I write it up.

SONNY
(stepping aside)
Get in there.

RANDI
What happened to you guys?

SONNY
I'll tell you after you write.

DEXTER
Boss?

SONNY
Yeah?

DEXTER
Break's over.

(DEXTER winks and nods, and SONNY gets the implication.)

SONNY
I gotta make a call. I'll be back.

(SONNY dashes out. RANDI commandeers his chair and takes control of his computer. DEXTER lingers in the middle of the room.)

RANDI
(with her back to Dexter)
Who's he calling?

DEXTER
I have no idea.

RANDI
Liar.

DEXTER
No, I really don't.

RANDI
What happened to you guys?

(DEXTER goes over to the office door, as if looking at SONNY's vapor trail.)

RANDI (cont.)
Dexter? What happened?

DEXTER
(after a long pause)
A lot of bad stuff.

(Blackout. End of scene.)

ACT THREE

SCENE SEVEN

(The scene opens with SONNY at his desk, facing out to the rest of the office. RANDI stands before the desk, a sheaf of papers in hand. DEXTER, also standing, lingers a bit out of their presence, against the far wall.)

SONNY
OK, read it.

(RANDI stands up straighter and lifts her papers to eye level. SONNY closes his eyes in concentration. DEXTER, noting this, does the same.)

RANDI
(reading)
Dillon Sloane, for nearly a decade the charismatic and occasionally controversial mayor of Montana's largest city, has engaged in a long-running conspiracy to funnel city monies into the hands of influential backers and his own companies, an investigation by the *Sun* has found.

SONNY

Good. Put the city and his job title up front. This won't be just a local story. Not after it gets out.

RANDI

If it gets out.

SONNY

When it gets out.

RANDI

I still don't see how you're going to pull that off.

SONNY

Faith, Randi. Have a little faith in the process.

DEXTER

Better to call it a "scheme" than a "conspiracy." No legal threshold to meet. If this ends up in court, he might not be charged with conspiracy if that's too hard to prove.

SONNY

Yes, good!

RANDI

OK, got it.

SONNY

Go on.

RANDI

(reading again)

Sloane, 47, has also been the subject of nearly a dozen complaints of unwelcome sexual advances toward female city staffers over the years, complaints that apparently were not followed up by the city's human resources department. In one case, the *Sun* has seen an email exchange among city staffers that suggested the complainant would, quote, "drop the matter expeditiously," quote, if confronted with her own flagging job performance and the possibility that she might be dismissed for cause.

SONNY

Dirty, manipulative sonsabitches.

RANDI
(*still reading*)
All told, the *Sun* has seen and has in its possession emails, ledgers, contemporaneous notes by city staffers, and articles of incorporation for a series of shell companies owned by Sloane that show the mayor, or his corporate concerns, have pocketed nearly $300,000 in city monies during his tenure. Companies owned by financial supporters of his two campaigns for office have pulled down nearly a half-million more dollars, some through competitive bidding but others through no-bid contracts.

SONNY
OK, that's good. I'll read the rest myself. Outstanding, Randi. Just outstanding. And you have notes, documents, and quotes from everyone who's on the record?

RANDI
Every single one. It's all in there and notated.

SONNY
Fucking fantastic job. Dexter?

DEXTER
Agreed. Fantastic.

RANDI
So we have a story.

SONNY
We have more than that. We have a goddamn exclusive.

RANDI
I'll say it again: Livingston will never let this see the light of day.

(*The phone on SONNY's desk rings. He rolls over in his chair and puts the speakerphone on.*)

SONNY
Talk to me.

MAN'S VOICE
Sonny, it's Jennings down in the production room.

SONNY

Hi, Dave.

MAN'S VOICE

(perplexed)
Yeah, hey. Listen, something's happened down here.

SONNY

Oh?

MAN'S VOICE

Yeah, there's been a break-in or something.

SONNY

Oh, no! Are you OK?

MAN'S VOICE

Yeah, yeah, we're fine, but…Jesus, it's a mess down here.

SONNY

What happened?

MAN'S VOICE

There's, like, six or eight crowbars jammed into the drums. My press rotors are all beat to hell. Somebody splashed goddamn house paint on the paper rolls and, jeez, I don't know, looks like they took a chainsaw to some of them. There's paper all over the damn place.

SONNY

Chainsaws? Are you sure?

MAN'S VOICE

Something like that. Who'd do this?

SONNY

I haven't the faintest.

(At this, RANDI and DEXTER, who have been listening in increasing wonder, exchange looks. RANDI is especially interested, as it's all news to her. They begin to titter, then smother the rising laughter.)

MAN'S VOICE

Thieves, I bet. They beat the outside door all to hell, too, which is where I imagine they came in. Spray-painted the security cameras. Wonder if they've been anywhere else in the building.

SONNY

I don't know. We haven't heard anything up at this end of the place.

MAN'S VOICE

What do you want me to do? Call Livingston? We ain't putting out a paper tonight, so…

SONNY

So that's the end, then.

MAN'S VOICE

Yeah, I guess so.

SONNY

Well, Dave, I'd say go on home, you and your crew. I'll let Livingston know what happened.

MAN'S VOICE

Maybe I ought to call the cops.

SONNY

And lose the rest of your night while they stumble around investigating? I mean, do what you want, but I'd let Livingston handle it if I were you. It's going to be an insurance matter, probably. Under the circumstances, he might just want to avoid the headache of police involvement, you know?

MAN'S VOICE

(skeptically)
Maybe.

SONNY

Tell you what: I'll call Livingston, then I'll do whatever he wants to do, OK? Go on home. You've earned it. Thanks for letting me know, Dave. And good luck to you.

MAN'S VOICE

Yeah, you, too, Sonny.

(SONNY disengages the phone.)

RANDI
Well, I certainly didn't see that coming.

DEXTER
It's asymmetrical warfare.

SONNY
(snapping)
That's exactly what it is.

RANDI
What are you guys talking about?

DEXTER
Never mind.

RANDI
So all day I've been worried that Livingston wouldn't let us print this in the paper, and it turns out we're not going to let Livingston print a paper at all.

SONNY
You're getting it. Keep going.

RANDI
But I don't get it.

DEXTER
Yeah, neither do I.

RANDI
And if you call Livingston now, best-case scenario is he's going to send us home, just like you sent Jennings and the press crew home. And that means our story dies.

SONNY
Quite probably. But I'm not calling Livingston just yet.

DEXTER
You're not?

SONNY

I'll call him right around six tonight, hopefully when he's sitting down to his nightly plate of arteriosclerosis. Right around the time you, dear Randi, will be appearing on TV screens all around town, reading this news. Right around the time the Channel 2 website will be putting up your story—our story—and beaming it to frontiers the Livingston Sloanes of the world can't possibly contain.

RANDI
(*gobsmacked*)
You cannot be serious.

SONNY

As the fucking heart attack I still might have before we're done. A *Sun*-Channel 2 joint exclusive! There's a job over there for you, too, if you want it. For you, too, Dexter. You remember Monica Thomas, Randi? You were her replacement here.

RANDI
(*still dazed*)
Yeah, I remember.

SONNY

Solid journalist. Runs the news operation over there. She said they'd be proud to have you. And seeing as I no longer have a place for you and your immense talents…

(*RANDI flings herself at SONNY, hugging him. DEXTER moves in for a handshake. SONNY allows the moment, then breaks things up.*)

SONNY

We don't have much time. Randi, go home first and put on something you'll want to be seen in on TV.

RANDI
(*muttering*)
Image-first TV numbskulls.

SONNY

Numbskulls who'll let you keep doing what you were born to do.

RANDI
I know, I know.

(SONNY turns to his desk and swipes his cellphone from it, fingers the keys, then holds it up as if pointing the camera lens at RANDI.)

SONNY
But first, a little something for the inevitable documentary film. Randi Hutch, what did you like about working at the *Sun*?

RANDI
(looking at the camera)
Afflicting the comfortable. Doing work that made a difference. Finding my way to the truth and making sure it wasn't hidden from everyone else. That's the short list.

(SONNY turns the lens toward Dexter.)

SONNY
And you, Dexter Collins?

DEXTER
I was here only a day.

SONNY
That's OK.

DEXTER
Best job I've ever had.

(This breaks SONNY and RANDI into laughter.)

DEXTER (cont.)
It was like getting a postgraduate degree in a matter of hours. Gratitude, man. That's all there is.

(SONNY, clearly pleased, hands the phone to RANDI.)

SONNY
OK, do me.

RANDI
Whenever you're ready.

SONNY
(his voice breaking)
Give me my Romeo; and, when he shall die, / Take him and cut him out in little stars, / And he will make the face of heaven so fine / That all the world will be in love with night / And pay no worship to the garish sun. … That's it. There's nothing more to say, and that's probably the last time I'll say it.

(RANDI closes out the phone and hands it back to him, then folds herself into his arms again. He holds her tenderly.)

SONNY
You gotta go now.

(They break the embrace. RANDI backs away, leans in for a quick hug with DEXTER, then heads for the door. Once in the doorway, she turns back and waves, then exits the stage.)

DEXTER
So we didn't need the pumpkin after all.

SONNY
Nope. Randi got the story, on the record, no anonymous sources. Clean and beautiful.

DEXTER
Will you ever tell me what you had on Max Duncan?

SONNY
Never. It didn't come up, we didn't need it, so I'll never part with it. I will say this: His failings and fears are of a moral nature, not a legal one. A pitiable bastard. I didn't want to hurt him.

DEXTER
I see.

SONNY
Please don't tell anyone I'm basically a softie.

DEXTER
Your secret is safe with me, sir.

SONNY
Good man.

(*DEXTER looks admiringly at SONNY.*)

DEXTER
You knew how it would all unfold, didn't you?

SONNY
Most of it, yeah.

DEXTER
From the very beginning?

SONNY
From the very beginning.

DEXTER
But do you know how it ends?

(*SONNY goes back to his desk, roots around underneath it, then comes up with a small tripod. He carries that to the long table in the middle of the office, sets it up, then affixes the cellphone to it, lining it up so the lens is pointed toward the door.*)

SONNY
Still figuring that part out.

DEXTER
No, you're not.

SONNY
No, I'm not.

(*SONNY checks the clock on the wall.*)

SONNY (cont.)
But it could still go either way, despite my figuring, couldn't it?

DEXTER
I guess so.

SONNY
We'd better wash up and change out of these clothes. We're walking crime scenes.

DEXTER
(looking himself over)
Yeah, a mess.

SONNY
Dex?

DEXTER
Yes, sir?

SONNY
Your mom's gonna be so proud of you.

DEXTER
(smiling big)
I know she is, sir.

(Blackout. End of scene.)

Interlude idea

To give the actors portraying SONNY and DEXTER time to do a costume change before Scene Eight, consider a projection of a quick-cuts series of major news events, captured in archival footage—moon landing, Watergate, Manson trial, shuttle disaster, great Olympic moments, etc., etc. A little visual feast, a little reminder of what it means to us to have moments captured, not just for our immediate information but also for our memories.

"You can crush a man with journalism."
William Randolph Hearst

SCENE EIGHT

(The scene opens in SONNY's office with SONNY and DEXTER in fresh clothes, casual, as if they were on their way to a barbecue rather than in an office. They're standing, watching a small TV set that has been placed on the long office table, facing away from the audience.)

SONNY
She'll be on after this commercial.

DEXTER
I'm nervous.

SONNY
(amused)
Like before a big game?

DEXTER
Worse. Way worse.

(SONNY claps a hand on DEXTER's shoulder, grips it, and smiles.)

SONNY
We've got a great game plan. It's going to be OK. I think we're going to win the championship.

DEXTER
Thanks.

(SONNY slips over to the desk and picks up the handset of the office phone, then dials a number. The conversation that ensues is one-sided; the audience hears only SONNY, with appropriate pauses where LIVINGSTON would be filling in with his lines.)

SONNY
Livingston, it's Sonny.

Yeah, we're almost done here.

Listen, turn on Channel 2.

I know you're eating, but turn it on. You need to see this.

Just wait a second.

Yeah, that's Randi Hutch. Now shut up and listen, OK?

You getting that?

(SONNY holds the handset away from his ear, and the audience hears incoherent anger. He then puts the handset to his ear again.)

Be sure to chew that steak fully. I don't want you to choke.

Well, that's the thing. There won't be a paper.

Who approved this? I approved it. I'm the editor, right?

Such language. I do believe if you carry on in this vein, Livingston, I will not be able to accept your letter of recommendation.

Oh yeah? Well, do what you think is right. You won't have to look for me.

(SONNY puts the handset back in the cradle.)

DEXTER
And so it begins.

SONNY
Nope. Here comes the ending you asked about.

DEXTER
He's coming down here?

SONNY
So he says. We've got a few minutes before things get stupid. Let's savor the moment.

(SONNY again roots through the drawers in his desk and scares up two shot glasses and a bottle of brown liquor. He sets the glasses down next to each other. DEXTER comes over for a closer look. SONNY opens the bottle and pours a shot into each glass.)

SONNY
When Livingston made me lay off my managing editor, I took on a new partner.

(SONNY shows the bottle proudly.)

SONNY (cont.)
Tuaca!

DEXTER
Never had it.

SONNY
We'll fix that.

DEXTER
Whatever you say, sir.

SONNY
How old are you?

DEXTER
Twenty-two.

SONNY
That's old enough!

DEXTER
Can I ask you something?

SONNY
Bring it.

DEXTER
What's going to happen here?

SONNY
I honestly don't know. But let me tell you something: That big tight end, he's wiggling his fingers.

(SONNY distributes the drinks, and he and DEXTER throw them back simultaneously. DEXTER is clearly stung by the potency, whereas SONNY licks his lips appreciatively.)

SONNY
(louder and more aggressively)
Tuaca!

(LIVINGSTON comes to the office doorway. DEXTER sees him first, and he taps SONNY's shoulder to draw his attention. LIVINGSTON steps into the office and stands menacingly. DEXTER falls back toward the table.)

LIVINGSTON
You son of a bitch.

SONNY
That's no way to talk to Dexter. You don't even know him.

LIVINGSTON
(explosively)
I'm talking to you, you lout!

SONNY
Well, that's no way to talk to me, either. It could hurt my feelings.

LIVINGSTON

When I'm through with you, hurt feelings will be the least of your worries, Sonny. I will fucking destroy you. I will take everything precious from you and—

SONNY

There's nothing precious left.

LIVINGSTON

—and when I'm through with you, when you have not a penny left, not a pot to piss in, not a place to lay your overlearned head, I will go after everyone you've ever cared about. Ruination!

(LIVINGSTON points at DEXTER.)

LIVINGSTON (cont.)

This one here, whoever he is, he's in trouble, too. Neither you nor he nor that bitch on TV will have another restful night's sleep in your whole pathetic lives.

SONNY

Well, the truth is, I don't sleep that well as it is, so…

LIVINGSTON

You keep talking, Sonny. I know what this is. Deflect, deflect, deflect. You're running out of room. You might as well be a dead man.

SONNY

Are you threatening me?

LIVINGSTON

I am.

SONNY

OK, that's it. No Christmas card for you.

LIVINGSTON

Just keep talking.

SONNY

I have nothing to say. Everything the *Sun* knows went out over Channel 2 tonight. And here's the part you can't handle: Every word of it was the truth.

Every single asserted fact. All true. Each of them uncovered by the hard work of the journalism you so clearly disdain. The story you thought you could kill actually lives. You can't win, Livingston, no matter what you do to me.

LIVINGSTON
Yeah, it's true. So what? Who cares if it's the truth?

SONNY
Somebody. Somebody will care. So go get fucked by an elk, you pernicious sack of pus.

(Something about the line enrages LIVINGSTON, who storms across the office toward SONNY, only to be taken down with a form-perfect tackle by DEXTER.)

LIVINGSTON
(in pain)
Jesus.

SONNY
Stay with him there, Dexter.

(DEXTER stands over the heap of LIVINGSTON, ready to put him down again. LIVINGSTON slowly, and painfully, sits up. DEXTER backs up a step or two. Meanwhile, SONNY gets the cellphone from the tripod.)

LIVINGSTON
(still woozy)
You're going to pay for that, both of you. You're going to pay big.

SONNY
No, I don't think we will. Self-defense against the raging of a temporarily insane man who had already threatened us with consequences both legal and physical, and all because we told the truth. Which he acknowledged.

LIVINGSTON
Says you.

SONNY
No, says you. Have a look at this.

(SONNY cues up a video from the phone and shows it to LIVINGSTON, whose eyes

grow wide at the mess he's made of things. LIVINGSTON tries to swipe the phone, but SONNY jerks it away.)

SONNY
Backed it up in the cloud. Don't even think about it.

(SONNY hands the phone to DEXTER, then goes to help LIVINGSTON to his feet. LIVINGSTON accedes to the help, then pushes SONNY away once he's up, but there's no vigor. He knows he's beaten.)

SONNY
It's been a hell of a day, Livingston. A hell of a day. You might want to go see what somebody's done to your production room.

LIVINGSTON
What?

SONNY
It's OK. You're just going to scrap everything anyway. You'll still be a very rich man in the morning. And I'll still be an out-of-work, unemployable news-paper editor. Go on home. We'll be gone soon. I'll leave the keys on the desk.

(LIVINGSTON trudges out. At the doorway, he encounters RANDI, who's coming in.)

LIVINGSTON
(half-heartedly)
You're fired.

RANDI
(in his face)
I know!

(LIVINGSTON shrinks from that and exits the stage. RANDI comes into the office and looks SONNY and DEXTER over.)

RANDI
Well, boys, how has your night gone?

(DEXTER pulls her into a half-hug. SONNY pulls out one of the office chairs and climbs atop it, standing.)

SONNY
Tonight, we put out the best fucking paper in the country. In the world!

(Blackout. End of scene.)

"I don't so much mind that newspapers are dying off. It's watching them commit suicide that pisses me off."
Molly Ivins

SCENE NINE

(The scene opens with SONNY, RANDI, and DEXTER at the door to SONNY's office, saying their goodbyes with handshakes and hugs.)

RANDI
I love you, Sonny.

SONNY
(cupping her cheeks)
I know you do. You'll get over that. Call me for coffee next week.

DEXTER
Thanks for the education. And the job offer. I think I'll go home to Massachusetts, though.

SONNY
They've got Livingston Sloanes out there, too, the wicked pissahs. Take them down, one at a time.

(After RANDI and DEXTER leave, SONNY lingers at the door, then at last falls back into the office. He straightens things up—chairs put where they belong, etc. He finds a box and starts loading up the contents of his desk. He turns the computer off. Something catches his attention, and he goes over to the back wall, finds the dartboard/family portrait, and hangs it up delicately, the family faces staring back at him. ANNA arrives at the office door.)

ANNA
Hi, Sonny.

(ANNA's voice wheels SONNY around. He smiles at her.)

SONNY
Hi, Anna.

(Each takes a step closer to the other.)

ANNA
I'm a little later than I said I'd be.

SONNY
You're right on time.

ANNA
I watched the news. Randi is really good, isn't she?

SONNY
She has potential.

ANNA
I had a stop to make before I came over. A message to deliver.

SONNY
(smiling)
I understand.

ANNA
You got your wish. It's over with Dillon.

SONNY
And you'll get yours. Did you bring the papers?

(ANNA reaches into her satchel and produces a stack. SONNY takes them, sets them on the table, whips out a pen, and signs. He hands the papers back to her.)

ANNA
Thank you. Well, goodbye, Sonny.

SONNY
Goodbye, Anna.

(ANNA turns to leave. When she gets to the door, she turns back to SONNY.)

ANNA
This was never my wish.

SONNY
Mine, either.

ANNA
Everything got so heavy, and I got so tired, and I looked around, and you weren't there and—

SONNY
I know.

ANNA
And I had to. Like the only way around it was through it, in the hardest possible way.

SONNY
I know. I'm so sorry. I disappeared on you, and that wasn't fair.

ANNA
Yes, you did.

SONNY
And I lost myself inside that grief, where I couldn't see how it was pummeling you.

ANNA
Yes, you did.

SONNY

I'm sorry.

ANNA

Well, are you found now?

SONNY

Not found, entirely. But I think I can see the way out now. Finally.

ANNA

I'm glad.

(ANNA turns away again, and SONNY walks up on her. When he begins speaking, she turns back and they're almost in the same space.)

SONNY

Sometimes, on a cold, clear night, the way it was when he left us, I sit in the living room of my little apartment, just me and the wind outside the window and the stars I can see, even here in town, and I think about him and how he's up there, in that heavenly glow. And the night goes on, and my endurance wanes, and sometimes, it's like he's found his way there into the room with me, just sitting across from me in the other chair, and he's looking at me. And I talk to him. I tell him I'm off his case for good about a haircut, that I regret every trivial thing I ever chewed on his ass about, that I didn't tell him more often how good he was and how proud I was. How proud I still am. I tell him about my day. I tell him anything that comes to mind, really, or nothing at all. I just speak it to him, to the air, because he's not really there, but morning is coming on and I've slipped time and distance and, I don't know, he could be there. Maybe he could. Maybe. If I wanted it bad enough. If I repented hard enough for failing him.

ANNA

Sometimes I step into his closet, straight into his shirts, and I smell him, and he is there. Some bit of him that's been left behind, it's there. I know it is.

SONNY

I'd sure like to experience that.

ANNA

Come over sometime. I'll cook a meal. You bring some wine. We'll find him together.

SONNY
Yeah?

ANNA
(smiling)
Yeah.

(SONNY puts a hand on the small of her back and escorts her through the door. They exit the stage together.)

(Blackout. End of scene. End of play.)

About the author

Casey Page

Craig Lancaster is the author of 10 novels, a collection of short stories, and two plays that have been produced on professional stages. His first full-length dramatic work, *Straight On To Stardust*, made its world premiere in October 2023 with Yellowstone Repertory Theatre.

His novels have made bestseller lists, have been translated widely, and have won awards internationally, nationally, and regionally, including two High Plains Book Awards (for *And It Will Be a Beautiful Life* and *600 Hours of Edward*).

In addition to his literary efforts, Lancaster is a research analyst with a specialty in money movement. He lives in Billings, Montana.